Storytime collection

p

Mrs Mouse's Holiday

Mrs Mouse was very excited. All year she had been *so* busy. First there had been nuts and berries to gather in readiness for winter. Then she had needed to give her little house a big spring clean to make it nice and fresh. Now, as the warm sun shone down on the trees and flowers of her woodland home, she had promised herself a well-deserved holiday. But getting ready for holidays seemed to make one busier than ever! There was so much to do!

First she took out her little case, opened it and placed it carefully on her neatly made bed. Then she rushed to her cupboard and selected some fine holiday dresses. Back to her case she scuttled and laid them in. Now she chose several pairs of shoes – a nice pair of sandals for walking along the front in, a pair of smart shoes for shopping in, an even smarter pair for going to dinner in, and another pair just in case!

"I'll need a couple of sun hats," she thought to herself, and so into the case they went as well. These were followed by a coat, some gloves and a scarf (just in case the breeze got up and it became cold). Then, in case it became very sunny, in went some sunglasses, some sun cream and a sunshade. But, oh dear, there were so many things in the case that it refused to shut. She tried sitting on it, and bouncing on it, but still it stubbornly would not close.

So out from the case came all the things that she had just put in, and Mrs Mouse scurried to the cupboard again and chose an even bigger case. This time they all fitted perfectly, and she shut the case with a big sigh of relief.

Now she was ready to go to the seaside for her holiday. She sat on the train, with her case on the rack above her head, munching her hazel nut sandwiches and looking eagerly out of the window hoping to see the sea. Finally, as the train chuffed around a bend, there it was! A great, deep blue sea shimmering in the sun, with white gulls soaring over the cliffs and headlands.

"I'm really looking forward to a nice, quiet rest," she said to herself.

Her guest house was very comfortable, and so close to the sea that she could smell the clean, salty air whenever she opened her window. "This is the life," she thought. "Nice and peaceful."

After she had put her clothes away, she put on her little swimming costume and her sun hat and packed her beach bag. Now she was ready for some peaceful sunbathing!

At the beach, she found herself a quiet spot, closed her eyes and was soon fast asleep. But not for long! A family of voles had arrived on the beach, and they weren't trying to have a quiet time at all. The youngsters in the family yelled at the top of their voices, splashed water everywhere, and sent their beach ball tumbling all over Mrs Mouse's neatly laid out beach towel.

Just as Mrs Mouse thought that it couldn't get any noisier, along came a crowd of ferrets. Now if you've ever sat on a beach next to a crowd of ferrets, you'll know what it's like. Their noisy shouting and singing made Mrs Mouse's head buzz.

Mrs Mouse couldn't stand it a moment longer. She was just wondering where she might find some peace and quiet when she spotted a rock just a little way out to sea.

"If I swim out to that rock," she thought, "I will surely have some peace and quiet there." So she gathered up her belongings and swam over to the rock. It was a bit lumpy, but at least it was quiet. Soon she was fast asleep again.

Just then the rock started to move slowly out to sea! It wasn't really a rock at all, you see, but a turtle which had been dozing near the surface. Off into the sunset it went, with Mrs Mouse dozing on its back, quite unaware of what was happening.

Eventually, the turtle came to a deserted island. At that moment, Mrs Mouse woke up. She looked at the empty beach, and without even knowing she had been sleeping on a turtle, she jumped off and swam to the shore, thinking it was the beach that she had just left.

Just then, the turtle swam off, and Mrs Mouse suddenly realised what had happened. For a moment she was horrified. But then she looked at the quiet, palm–fringed beach with no-one about but herself, and thought of the noisy beach she had just left.

"Well, perhaps this isn't such a bad place to spend a quiet holiday after all," she thought.

And that's just what she did. Day after day she lazed on her own private beach with no–one to disturb her. There were plenty of coconuts and fruits to eat, and she wanted for nothing. She even made herself a cozy bed from palm leaves.

Eventually, though, she started to miss her own little house in the woods and decided it was time to get back home. First she took half a coconut and nibbled out the tasty inside. "That will make a fine boat to sit in," she said.

Next she found a palm leaf and stuck it in the bottom of the shell. She took her little boat to the water's edge and, as the wind caught her palm leaf sail, off she floated back to the boarding house to get her belongings.

As she sailed back she thought, "This is the quietest holiday I've ever had. I may come back here next year!"

The Lost Lion

Once there was a lion cub called Lenny. He was a very tiny lion cub, but he was sure that he was the bravest lion in all of Africa. When his mother taught her cubs how to stalk prey, Lenny would stalk his own mother and pounce on her. When she showed them how to wash themselves, Lenny licked his sister's face instead so that she growled at him. When the mother lioness led her cubs down to the watering hole to drink, he jumped into the water and created a huge splash that soaked everyone.

The other lionesses were not amused. "You'd better watch that son of yours," they said to Lenny's mother, "or he'll get into really big trouble."

One day the mother lioness led her cubs on their first big hunt. "Stay close to me," she said, "or you could get hurt." She crawled off through the undergrowth with her cubs following on behind, one after the other. Lenny was at the back. The grass tickled his tummy and he wanted to laugh, but he was trying hard to be obedient. So he crawled along, making sure he kept the bobbing tail of the cub in front in sight. On and on they crawled until Lenny was beginning to feel quite weary.

"But a brave lion cub doesn't give up," he thought to himself. And on he plodded.

At last the grass gave way to a clearing. Lenny looked up, and to his dismay he saw that the tail he had been following was attached, not to one of his brothers or sisters, but to a baby elephant!

Somewhere along the trail he had started following the wrong tail and now he was hopelessly lost. He wanted to cry out for his mother but then he remembered that he was the bravest lion in all of Africa. So what do you think he did? He went straight up to the mother elephant and growled his fiercest growl at her. "That'll frighten her!" thought Lenny. "She won't dare growl back!" And, of course, she didn't growl back. Instead she lifted her trunk and trumpeted so loudly at Lenny that he was blown off his feet and through the air and landed against the hard trunk of a tree.

Lenny got up and found that his knees were knocking. "Oh my," he thought, "that elephant has a very loud growl. But I'm still definitely the bravest lion in all of Africa." He set off across the plain. It was getting hot in the midday sun and soon Lenny began to feel sleepy. "I think I'll just take a nap in that tree," he thought, and started climbing up into the branches.

To his surprise, he found that the tree was already occupied by a large leopard. "I'll show him who's boss," thought Lenny, baring his tiny claws. The leopard raised his head to look at Lenny, and then bared his own huge, razor-sharp claws. He took a swipe at Lenny with his paw. Without even touching Lenny, the wind from the leopard's great paw swept Lenny out of the tree and he landed with a bump on the ground.

Lenny got up and found that his legs were trembling. "Oh my," he thought, "that leopard had big claws. But I'm still definitely the bravest lion in Africa." He set off again across the plain. After a while he began to feel quite hungry. "I wonder what I can find to eat," he thought. Just then he saw a spotted shape lying low in the grass. "That looks like a tasty meal," thought Lenny as he pounced on the spotted shape.

But the spotted shape was a cheetah! Quick as a flash, the cheetah sprang away and as he did so, his tail caught Lenny a blow that sent him spinning round and round in circles.

When Lenny stopped spinning, he got up and found that his whole body was shaking. "Oh my," he thought, "that cheetah is a fast runner." Then he added in rather a small voice, "But I'm still the bravest lion in Africa." He set off again across the plain. By now it was getting dark and Lenny was wishing he was at home with his mother and brothers and sisters. "I wonder if they've noticed I've gone," he thought sadly as a tear rolled down his furry cheek. He felt cold and tired and hungry as he crawled into the undergrowth to sleep.

Some time later Lenny was woken by a noise that was louder than anything he'd ever heard before – louder even than the elephant's trumpeting. It filled the night air and made the leaves on the trees shake. The noise was getting louder and louder and the animal that was making it was getting nearer and nearer. Lenny peeped out from his hiding place and saw a huge golden creature with big yellow eyes that shone in the dark like lamps. It had a great crown of shaggy golden fur all around its head and its red jaws were open wide revealing a set of very large white fangs. How it roared! Lenny was terrified and about to turn tail and run, when the animal stopped roaring and spoke to him. "Come here, Lenny," said the animal gently. "It's me, your father, and I'm going to take you home. Climb up on my back, little one."

So Lenny climbed up on his father's back and was carried all the way home. And when they got there his father told his mother and his brothers and sisters that Lenny had been a very brave lion after all.

The Bee Who Wanted More Stripes

Bertie the bee was a rather vain young bee. Every morning, as soon as he woke up, he would find a large dewdrop in which to admire his reflection. The thing that Bertie liked best about himself was his stripes. He thought stripes were the smartest, flashiest fashion accessory any animal could have. He just wished he had more stripes. But he only had a couple. "Still," he thought, "they are very fine stripes."

Then he had an idea. What if he could get some more stripes? He would be the stripiest bee around, and then everyone else would admire him, too. "I know what I'll do," he said. "I'll ask some other very stripy animals how they got all their stripes, and maybe I can copy them."

He buzzed off through the wood, looking for striped animals to ask. He flew across the fields and then the sea and at last he reached a place where there seemed to be quite a few striped animals. The first animal he approached looked like a striped horse. "Hello, neddy!" said Bertie, landing on the beast's nose.

"I'm not a horse – I'm a zebra. And get off my nose!" said the zebra crossly.

"I do beg your pardon," said Bertie. "I just wanted to ask you how you got your stripes."

"Well," said the zebra, "I used to be all brown. Then one day I came across a piano in the middle of the plain. As I walked past the piano, its black and white keys started to play a tune all by themselves. Then I looked down and found I had turned black and white, too. And if you believe that you'll believe anything!" And with that the zebra laughed and trotted off.

Bertie continued on his way. Now he could see a large striped cat. "Hello, puss!" said Bertie, landing on the creature's back.

"I'm not a cat – I'm a tiger. And get off my back!" growled the tiger.

"I'm so sorry," said Bertie, "I just wanted to ask you how you got your stripes."

"Well," said the tiger, "I used to be all yellow. Then one day, when I was a cub, I was playing with a ball of black string and I got all tangled up in it. And that's how I got my stripes. And if you believe that you'll believe anything!" And the tiger started to laugh as he stalked off.

Bertie continued on his way. Soon he could see a long striped worm slithering through the grass. "Hello, little worm!" called Bertie, landing on the worm's tail.

"I'm not a worm – I'm a snake. And get off my tail!" hissed the snake.

"Oh dear. I didn't mean to upset you," said Bertie. "I just wanted to ask you how you got your stripes."

"Well," said the snake, "I used to be all brown. Then one day I was crossing a road just as the traffic lights were changing from red to green, and when I reached the other side I found that I was striped red and green from head to tail. And if you believe that you'll believe anything!" And the snake started to laugh as he slithered away.

Bertie continued on his way once more. Then he spotted a squirrel with a striped tail in a tree. "Hello, squirrel!" he said, landing on the animal's paw.

"I'm not a squirrel – I'm a ring-tailed lemur. And get off my paw!" said the ring-tailed lemur angrily.

"I do apologise," said Bertie. "I just wanted to ask you how you got your striped tail."

"Well," said the ring-tailed lemur, "my tail used to be all white. Then one day I was playing hoop-la with my friends. I said they could use my tail as a target, and so they threw all the rings on to my tail. But they got stuck. And that's how I got a striped tail. And if you believe that you'll believe anything!" And the ring-tailed lemur started to laugh as he scampered away.

"Well," thought Bertie, "I'd better give it a go!" First he looked for a piano on the plain, but to no avail. There just wasn't a piano to be found. Then he looked for a ball of string – but he couldn't find one of those, either. He did find a set of traffic lights and he buzzed backwards and forwards in front of them until he felt quite dizzy, but he still had the same number of stripes. Finally, he called out, "Anyone fancy a game of hoop-la?" But there was no reply. It was night time and all the animals were asleep.

"I'll just have to make my way home," thought Bertie sadly. He flew all through the night and arrived home exhausted in the morning.

Just then he met Clarice, the wise old bee. "Clarice," said Bertie, "I really would like some more stripes, but although I've asked lots of stripy animals how they got their stripes, all they gave me were silly answers."

Clarice looked at Bertie rather sternly and said, "You only get the stripes you were born with, Bertie. And besides, do you know what you would be if you had more stripes? You would be a wasp!"

Bertie looked horrified. The last thing he wanted to be was a wasp. Wasps were always going around frightening and stinging everyone, and no-one liked them at all.

Bertie thought for a few moments and then said, "Perhaps having just a few stripes but being liked by others is better after all."

The Missing Scarf

Kanga was very proud of her stripy knitted scarf. She had made it herself and she had also made a smaller matching one for her son, Joey. Kanga used to hop through the bush with her scarf streaming out behind her, while Joey's could just be seen poking out of the top of her pouch. Now Joey was older, he was too big for Kanga's pouch, but he still wore his scarf as he hopped along beside his mother.

Then one day Kanga woke up to find that her beautiful scarf was missing. She searched high and low but it was nowhere to be found. Eventually she decided that she would have to go out into the bush to look for it.

"Stay here," she said to Joey. "I'll try not to be long. I'm sure to find my scarf soon." Kanga hopped off into the bush and started to search among the roots of trees and under stones.

She had gone quite a long way when, looking up into the branches of a eucalyptus tree, she spotted Koala. Now Koala was usually to be found asleep, but this time she was busy preparing a meal of eucalyptus leaves for her children. Kanga looked up at Koala and then her jaw dropped. For Koala was quite clearly wearing Kanga's scarf around her tummy. Then, to Kanga's horror, she saw Koala use the end of the scarf to wipe the teacups! "Koala," Kanga called. "Whatever do you think you're doing?"

Koala stopped cleaning the teacups and looked down through the branches of the eucalyptus tree at Kanga. "I'm wiping my teacups with my apron," she replied sleepily, "and I'll thank you not to interfere!" And with that, she yawned and moved several branches further up the tree.

21

Poor Kanga felt very embarrassed. How could she have mistaken Koala's striped apron for her own scarf? She hopped away and carried on further into the bush. After a while she could hear Kookaburra's familiar laughing call nearby. "I know," thought Kanga, "I'll ask her if she's seen my scarf. She'd be able to spot it easily from up in the sky." She followed the sound of Kookaburra's call until she came to the tree where she lived. She looked up and, sure enough, there was Kookaburra flying towards the tree. Kanga was about to call up when her jaw dropped again. For Kookaburra was quite clearly carrying Kanga's scarf in her beak. "Kookaburra," Kanga called. "Whatever do you think you're doing?"

"I'm lining my nest," mumbled Kookaburra through a beakful of stripy feathers. "And I'll thank you not to interfere," she added more distinctly, for she had now reached the nest and was arranging the feathers carefully in place.

22

Poor Kanga felt even more embarrassed. How could she have mistaken the feathers for her own scarf? She hopped away and carried on further into the bush. After a while she reached a wide open plain and there she saw Emu running past with his baby chicks on his back. As he rushed past, Kanga's jaw dropped yet again. For Emu quite clearly had Kanga's scarf tucked in among his chicks. "Emu," called Kanga. "Whatever do you think you're doing?"

"I'm taking my chicks to safety," said Emu, glancing up at the sky as he sped away. "And you'd be wise to do the same," he added. Then Kanga realised that what she had thought was her rolled-up scarf were just the striped chicks on Emu's back.

Poor Kanga felt even more embarrassed. How could she have made such a mistake? Then she felt a few spots of rain on her nose and, looking up, saw a huge black cloud overhead. There was no time to lose – she must find shelter.

She made a dash for some trees at the edge of the plain and soon found herself by a stream. She wandered along beside the stream feeling cold, wet, tired and miserable. Finally, she lay down in the wet grass beside the stream and tried to get to sleep. She shivered with cold and wondered how Joey was and whether he was behaving himself. She so hoped he hadn't got into mischief.

Just then there was a tap on her shoulder and there stood Platypus. "I could hear you in my burrow over there," she said pointing towards a hole beside the stream just above the water. "I thought you might like this to keep you warm," she added.

"My scarf!" exclaimed Kanga.

"Oh, is that what it is? I'm ever so sorry," said Platypus. "I've been using it as a blanket for my babies. It's rather cold and damp in my burrow, you know," she added, rather forlornly.

"Where did you find it?" asked Kanga.

"It was stuck on some thorns and I know I shouldn't have taken it, but I just thought it would be so nice for keeping my young ones warm," blurted Platypus, and she started to sob.

"There now," said Kanga, "don't cry. You can keep the scarf. You need it more than me."

Platypus stopped crying and looked overjoyed. "Thank you," she said.

"No, thank you," said Kanga. "I've learned a lesson, which is not to get upset over a scarf, for I've ended up falling out with my friends."

Kanga made her way back home, but it took a long time because she apologised to all her friends on the way. When she explained what had happened Emu, Kookaburra and Koala all forgave her, and by the time she reached home she was feeling much better. Joey was there to greet her. "What have you been up to while I was away?" she asked.

"I made you this," he said. He handed her a scarf. It was a very funny-looking scarf, made out of twigs, grass and feathers, but Kanga loved it very much.

"This is much more special than my old scarf," she said. And she gave Joey an extra big hug.

Mr Mole Gets Lost

Mr Mole poked his little black nose out from the top of one of his mole hills and gave a great big sniff of the air. Then he sniffed again. And then a third time just to make sure. "Oh dear," he thought, "it smells like it's going to rain."

Mr Mole didn't like the rain one bit. Every time he got caught in the rain his plush little velvet fur coat got all wet and drippy, and he left muddy footprints all over his underground burrow. But worse still, the rain got in through the holes in his mole hills and then everything got all soggy and took days to dry out.

Well, the skies got darker and darker, and very soon little spots of rain began to fall. Then the spots became bigger. And then bigger still. Before long, all you could see before your eyes were big, straight rods of rain bouncing off the leaves on the trees, pounding the ground and turning everything muddy and wet.

Mr Mole had never seen rain like it. He sat in his burrow in the middle of the meadow wishing it would stop. But it just kept raining and raining. Soon the rain started entering his burrow. First it went drip, drip, drip through the holes in his mole hills, and then it became a little river of water in the bottom of his burrow. Then the little river became a bigger, faster-flowing river and suddenly Mr Mole was being washed along by it. Through the tunnels of his burrow he went, this way and then that, as the water gushed and poured through his underground home.

The next thing he knew he was being washed out of his burrow completely as the rain water carried him off down the meadow. Down he went, not knowing which way up he was or where he was going. Now he was being washed through the woods at the bottom of the meadow, but still the water carried him on, bouncing and turning him until he was dizzy and gasping for breath.

Suddenly, he came to a halt. The rain water gurgled and trickled around him and then flowed onwards, as he found himself stuck firmly in the branches of a bush. "Oh dear," Mr Mole said as he got himself free. "Goodness me, where can I be?" he thought. Mr Mole looked around him, but being a very short-sighted mole – as most moles are – he couldn't make out any of the places that were familiar to him. Worse still, he couldn't smell any smells that were familiar to him. He was completely lost, far from home, and had no idea how to get back again. Now, to make things worse, it was starting to get dark.

"Woo-oo-oo-oo-oo!" said a voice suddenly. Mr Mole nearly jumped out of his moleskin with fright. "I wouldn't stay here if I were you," said the voice again. Mr Mole looked up and found himself face to face with an enormous owl. "Don't you know it's not safe in the woods at night?" asked the owl. "There are snakes and foxes and weasels and all sorts of nasty creatures that you really wouldn't like to meet."

"Oh dear!" was all Mr Mole could think of saying. He told the owl of his terrible watery journey and how he was lost and didn't know how to get back home again.

"You need to talk to Polly Pigeon," said the owl. "She is a homing pigeon and she lives near your meadow. She can show you the way home. But we'll have to find her first. Stay close to me, mind, and look out for those snakes, foxes and weasels I told you about."

Mr Mole didn't need telling twice. He stayed so close to the kindly owl that every time the owl stopped or turned round to talk to Mr Mole, Mr Mole bumped right into him!

Through the dark, dangerous woods they went. Every now and again, there would be an unfriendly noise, such as a deep growl or a hiss, coming from the dense, tangled trees, but Mr Mole didn't want to think about that too much, so he just made sure that he never lost sight of the owl.

Finally, just when Mr Mole thought that he couldn't go a step further, they came to a halt by an old elm tree.

"Hallo-oooo," called the owl.

They were in luck. Polly Pigeon was waking up, and they found her just in time for she was about to continue her journey home.

"Please," said Mr Mole, "I'm afraid I'm terribly lost and don't know how to get back to my meadow. Will you take me there?"

"Of course I will," said Polly Pigeon. "We'd better let you rest here a while first, though. But we must go before it gets light."

So Mr Mole was soon trudging wearily back to his meadow, following as closely behind Polly Pigeon as he was able. Just as the first rays of sun lit the morning sky, Mr Mole smelled a very familiar smell. It was his meadow! He was almost home!

Soon, he was back in his own burrow. It was so wet and muddy, however, that the first thing he did was build some new tunnels higher up the meadow so that the rain wouldn't wash down into them so easily. Then he settled down to eat one of his supplies of worms, and fell into a deep, well-earned slumber.

The Wolf and the Seven Goats

There was once an old mother goat who had seven little goats. They all lived in a tiny house on the edge of a big, dark forest. One day, the mother goat had to go into the forest to collect food. Before she left, she called her seven little goats to her and said, "Now, children, promise me that while I am away you will lock the door and be on your guard against the wicked wolf. If you see him, don't let him in, because he would certainly eat you all up. You can recognize him by his gruff voice and his big black paws."

"Yes, mother," the little goats replied, "we promise to be very careful."

So the mother goat trotted cheerfully away into the forest, and the little goats locked the door. Some time later, there was a knock at the door, and the little goats heard a voice calling, "Open the door, children, it is your mother. I have brought back a present for each of you."

But the little goats heard that the voice was gruff, and not the gentle voice of their mother, and so they called, "No, we will not let you in! You do not have a soft voice like our mother's, you have a gruff voice. You are the wolf!"

So the cunning wolf went to a shop and stole a jar of syrup and swallowed it to make his voice soft. Then back he went to the little house by the forest. "Open the door, children," he called in his new, soft voice. "It is your mother. I have brought back a present for each of you."

Now the little goats heard the soft voice, but in his eagerness to get into the house the wolf had put his big black paws on to the window ledge, and so the little goats cried out, "No, we will not let you in! Our mother has beautiful white feet, but you have black feet. You are the wolf!"

So the wolf ran back into the village and went to the baker's shop, where he stole some flour and covered his paws in it. The wolf ran back to the little house by the forest. "Children, children, open the door!" he called again. "It is your mother. I have brought back a present for each of you."

The little goats heard the soft voice but they could not see any paws, and they called out, "Let us see your paws so that we know you really are our mother." So the wolf lifted up his paws, which of course were all white from the flour plastered on them. The little goats thought that this time it really was their mother, and they unlocked the door.

The wolf rushed in. The little goats screamed and tried to hide. One jumped into a drawer; the second squeezed under the bed; the third buried itself in the bedclothes; the fourth leaped into a cupboard; the fifth went into the oven; the sixth hid under a basin; and the littlest one slipped inside the grandfather clock. But the wolf found them and gobbled them up – all except the youngest one hiding in the grandfather clock. When the wolf had finished his meal, he felt very full and very sleepy. He wandered out of the house into a nearby meadow, lay down on some dry leaves, and promptly fell asleep.

When the mother goat came home from the forest, imagine her horror as she saw the door open, the furniture strewn around the house and the little goats all gone. She started calling them by name, but nobody answered until she called out the name of the youngest little goat, who was still hiding in the grandfather clock. She quickly pulled him out, and then he told her what had happened to all his brothers and sisters.

She ran out of the house with the little goat trotting beside her and soon found the wolf sleeping in the meadow. She looked carefully at him and saw that there were six lumps in his fat stomach, and that they seemed to be moving. "My little goats are still alive," she exclaimed with joy.

Quickly she sent the youngest goat back to her house for scissors, needle and thread. Then, while the wolf was still sleeping, she carefully cut a hole in the wolf's stomach. Soon a little goat popped out and then another and another, until all six were free and jumping for joy. They had not come to any harm, for in his greed the wolf had swallowed them all whole.

"Quick," cried the mother goat, "fetch me some rocks from the river so that I can fill up this wicked wolf's stomach." So the little goats each fetched a rock and the mother goat sewed them up inside the wolf's stomach.

When the wolf awoke, he was very thirsty. "What is the matter with me?" he thought. "I shouldn't have eaten all those goats at once. Now I've got indigestion." He set out to drink from the river. But his stomach was so heavy he could hardly walk and he staggered to the water's edge. As he bent over to drink, the weight of the stones pulled the wolf into the water, where he sank straight to the bottom and drowned. Then the mother goat and all her little goats – who had been watching – danced for joy. For never again would they be afraid of the wicked wolf!

The Greedy Hamster

There was once a hamster named Harry. He was a very greedy hamster. As soon as his food was put in his cage he gobbled it all up, and then he would push his little nose through the bars in the hope that something else to eat might come within reach. From his cage he could see all manner of delicious food on the kitchen table – and the smells! The scent of freshly baked bread was enough to send him spinning round in his exercise wheel with frustration.

"It's not fair!" he grumbled to himself. "They're all eating themselves silly out there and here am I simply starving to death!" (At this point he would usually remember the large meal he had just eaten and that his tummy was indeed still rather full.)

"If only I could get out of this beastly cage, I could feast on all the food I deserve," he announced to himself, and the thought of all those tasty morsels made his mouth water.

One night after the family had gone to bed, Harry was having one last spin in his wheel before retiring to his sawdust mattress. As he spun around, he heard an unfamiliar squeaky noise.

"That's funny," thought Harry. "The little girl oiled my wheel only today. It surely can't need oiling again." He stopped running and got off the wheel, but the squeak continued. Harry sat quite still on his haunches and listened intently. Then he realised it was the door to his cage squeaking. The door! The door was flapping open. The little girl had not closed it properly before she went to bed. Harry did a little dance of glee. Then he went to the door and looked cautiously out in case there was any danger. But all seemed to be well. The cat was asleep on a chair. The dog was sleeping soundly on the floor.

Now, as well as being a greedy hamster, Harry was also clever. Once outside the cage, the first thing he did was look at the catch to see how it worked. Yes! He was pretty sure he could work out how to open it from the inside now. Harry sniffed the air. There were some tasty titbits left over from a birthday party on the table. He could smell the sugar icing, and soon he was on the table, cramming his mouth with odds and ends of cheese sandwiches and pieces of chocolate cake. When he had eaten his fill, he stuffed his cheek pouches with ginger biscuits and ran back into his cage, closing the door behind him.

"Good!" thought Harry. "Now I will never be hungry again."

The next night Harry let himself out of his cage and helped himself to food, and again the next night and the night after that. He feasted on everything and anything – nuts, bananas, pieces of bread, left-over jelly and slices of pizza were all pushed into his greedy mouth. Each time he returned to his cage he filled his cheeks with more and more food. He did not notice that he was getting fatter and fatter, although he was aware that he could no longer run round in his wheel without falling off! Then one night, he undid the door catch but found he was simply too wide to get through the door!

For a while Harry sat in a very bad temper in the corner of the cage. His cheeks were still bulging with food from his last midnight feast, but the greedy hamster wanted more. Then he had an idea. "I'll get that lazy cat to help," he thought. He squealed at the top of his voice until the cat, who had been dreaming of rats, woke up with a start.

"What do you want?" she hissed at Harry. Harry explained his problem.

"Of course, I'd be only too pleased to help," said the crafty cat, thinking to herself here was an extra dinner! With her strong claws she bent back the door frame of the cage, until there was just enough room for Harry to squeeze through. Then, with a mighty swipe of her paw, she caught him and gobbled him whole. She felt extremely full, what with Harry and all his food inside her. She could barely crawl back to her chair and soon she was fast asleep again and snoring loudly with her mouth open. Inside her tummy Harry, too, felt very uncomfortable. Every time the cat snored, it sounded like a thunderstorm raging around his head.

"I must get out of here," he thought, and headed for the cat's open jaws. But he was far too fat to get out again. Then he had another idea. Through the cat's jaws he could see the dog lying on the floor.

"Help! Help!" he squeaked. The dog woke up to a very strange sight. There was the cat lying on the chair snoring, but she also seemed to be squeaking, "Help!" The dog put his head on one side. He was very perplexed. Then he saw a pair of beady eyes and some fine whiskers inside the cat's mouth. It was Harry!

"Get me out of here, please," pleaded Harry.

Now the dog did not very much like the cat, so he was quite willing to help the hamster.

"I'll stick my tail in the cat's mouth. Then you hang on while I pull you out," said the dog. "But mind you don't make a sound and wake the cat, or she'll surely bite my tail!" The dog gingerly put the tip of his tail inside the cat's open jaws, just far enough for Harry's little paws to grab hold. Then he pulled with all his might. Out popped Harry and out of Harry popped all the food he'd stored in his cheeks – peanuts, an apple core and a slice of jam tart!

"Thank you, thank you," gasped Harry as he made a dash for his cage and slammed the door shut. "I think I'll stay in my cage from now on and just stick to the food I'm given!"

Mr Squirrel Won't Sleep

It was autumn. The leaves were falling from the trees in the forest and there was a cold nip in the air. All the animals began to get ready for winter.

One night Mr Fox came back from hunting and said to his wife, "There's not much food about now it's getting colder. We'd better start storing what we can to help tide us over the winter."

"You're right, Mr Fox," replied his wife, as she gathered her cubs into their lair.

"I'd love to go fishing," said Mr Bear, "but I'll have to wait until spring now." He went into his den, shut the door tight and sealed it.

"Well, I'm off for a holiday in the sun," announced Mrs Cuckoo, preening her feathers. "See you all next year!" she called as she took to the wing and flew south.

Mrs Mouse ran by with a mouthful of straw. "Must dash," she squeaked, "or my winter bed will never be finished in time." But soon she, too, was curled up with her tail wrapped around her for warmth.

Now only Mr Squirrel wasn't ready for winter. He danced about in his tree, leaping from branch to branch and chasing his tail. "Ha, ha!" he boasted. "I don't have to get ready for winter. I have a fine store of nuts hidden away, a beautiful bushy tail to keep me warm and besides, I don't feel in the least bit sleepy." And he carried on playing in his tree.

"Are you still awake?" snapped Mr Fox.

"Go to sleep!" growled Mr Bear.

"Please be quiet," squeaked Mrs Mouse, drawing her tail more tightly about her ears.

But Mr Squirrel wouldn't go to sleep. Not a bit of it. He danced up and down all the more and shouted, "I'm having SUCH FUN!" at the top of his voice.

Winter came. The wind whistled in the trees' bare branches, the sky turned grey and it became bitterly cold. Then it started to snow. At first Mr Squirrel had a grand time making snowballs – but there was no-one around to throw them at and he began to feel rather lonely. Soon he felt cold and hungry, too.

"No problem!" he said to himself. "I'll have some nice nuts to eat. Now, where did I bury them?" He scampered down his tree to find that the ground was deep with snow. He ran this way and that trying to find his hiding places, but all the forest looked the same in the snow and soon he was hopelessly lost.

"Whatever shall I do?" he whimpered, for now he was shivering with cold and hunger and his beautiful, bushy tail was all wet and bedraggled.

All of a sudden he thought he heard a small voice. But where was it coming from? He looked all around but there was no sign of anyone. Then he realised that the voice was coming from under the snow. "Hurry up!" said the voice. "You can join me down here, but you'll have to dig a path to my door."

Mr Squirrel started digging frantically with his front paws and sure enough there was a path leading to a door under a tree stump. The door was slightly open – open enough for Mr Squirrel to squeeze his thin, tired body through.

Inside was a warm, cosy room with a roaring fire, and sitting by the fire was a tiny elf. "I heard you running around up there and thought you might be in need of a bit of shelter," said the elf. "Come and warm yourself by the fire." Mr Squirrel was only too pleased to accept and soon he was feeling warm and dry.

"This isn't my house, you know," said the elf. "I think it might be part of an old badgers' sett. I got lost in the forest and so when I found this place, I decided to stay here until spring. Though how I'll ever find my way home, I don't know." A fat tear rolled down the elf's cheek.

"I have been a very foolish squirrel," said Mr Squirrel. "If you hadn't taken me in I surely would have died. I am indebted to you and if you will let me stay here until spring, I will help you find your way home."

"Of course you can stay," replied the elf. "I'd be glad of the company." So Mr Squirrel settled down with his tail for a blanket and soon he was fast asleep.

Days and nights passed, until one day the elf popped his head out of the door and exclaimed, "The snow has melted, spring is coming. Wake up, Mr Squirrel." Mr Squirrel rubbed his eyes and looked out. It was true. There were patches of blue in the sky and he could hear a bird singing.

"Climb upon my back," Mr Squirrel said to the elf. "I'm going to show you the world." They set off through the forest until they came to the highest tree of all.

"Hold tight!" called Mr Squirrel as he climbed up through the branches until finally they reached the very top of the tree.

"You can look now," said Mr Squirrel, seeing that the elf had put his tiny hands over his eyes. The elf uncovered his eyes and stared and stared. He had never seen anything like it in his whole life. Stretching in all directions, as far as the eye could see, were mountains, lakes, rivers, forests and fields.

"What's that silvery-blue thing in the distance?" asked the elf.

"Why, that's the sea!" replied Mr Squirrel.

Suddenly the elf started to jump for joy.

"What is it?" said Mr Squirrel.

"I… I… can see my home," cried the elf, pointing down into the valley below the forest. "And there's my wife sitting in a chair in the sunshine. I must go home, Mr Squirrel. Thank you for showing me the world, for I should never have seen my home again without you." And with that he climbed down the tree and skipped all the way home.

Mr Squirrel made his way back to his own tree.

"Where have you been?" said Mr Fox.

"We've been looking for you," said Mr Bear.

"I'm glad you're home," said Mrs Mouse.

"So am I," said Mr Squirrel. "I've been very foolish, but I've learned my lesson. Now let's have a party – I've got rather a lot of nuts that need eating up!"

So the animals celebrated spring with a fine feast.

And Mr Squirrel vowed not to be silly again next winter.

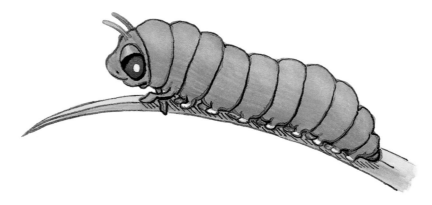

The Jealous Caterpillar

One spring day a green caterpillar sat on a leaf. He watched a beautiful butterfly flutter past him on the breeze. "It's not fair. Here I am stuck on this boring leaf with nothing to do and nowhere to go while that lucky creature can fly across the world and see far-off lands," thought the caterpillar crossly. "And what's more," he continued to himself, "not only has that butterfly got wings with which to fly, but he's beautiful, too. Look at poor me. I'm just a dull green. No-one will notice me because I'm the same colour as the leaf." The caterpillar really did feel very sorry for himself, and rather jealous. "Go and enjoy yourself. Don't worry about me," he called spitefully to the butterfly.

But the butterfly hadn't heard a single word the caterpillar had been muttering, and soon he flew away. The caterpillar suddenly decided that he was going to be like the butterfly. "I'll learn how to fly and I'll paint myself lovely colours so that I look beautiful, too," he thought. He looked around for something to paint himself with but, of course, there was nothing at all on the leaf. Then he tried to fly. He launched himself from his leaf and tried to flap his tail, but all he did was land on the leaf below.

Along came a ladybird. "Aha!" thought the caterpillar. "Here's a beautiful creature who knows how to fly. I'll ask her to teach me." So the caterpillar said, "Hello, I've been admiring your beautiful wingcase. Could you tell me how I, too, could be beautiful? And can you teach me to fly?"

The ladybird looked at the caterpillar. "Be patient and wait a while," she said wisely, "and soon enough you'll get what you want." And with that the ladybird went on her way.

"Whatever can she mean? She's just too proud to teach me," the caterpillar thought jealously.

Some time later a bee buzzed past and landed on a nearby leaf. "Aha!" thought the caterpillar. "Here's a beautiful creature who knows how to fly. I'll ask him to teach me." So the caterpillar said, "Hello, I've been admiring your beautiful striped back. Could you tell me how I, too, could be beautiful? And can you teach me to fly?"

The bee looked at the caterpillar. "You'll find out soon enough, young man," said the bee sternly. And with that he went on his way.

"Whatever can he mean? He's just too haughty to teach me," the caterpillar thought jealously.

Now a while later along came a bird. "Aha!" thought the caterpillar once more. "Here's a beautiful creature who knows how to fly. I'll ask him to teach me." So once again the caterpillar said, "Hello, I've been admiring your beautiful feathers. Could you tell me how I, too, could be beautiful? And can you teach me to fly?"

The bird looked at the caterpillar and thought to himself slyly that here was a very silly caterpillar, but he would make a tasty snack for his chicks. "Let's see if I can trick him," he thought.

"I can't give you wings and I can't make you beautiful. But I can show you the world. I expect you'd like to see the world, wouldn't you, little caterpillar?" said the bird.

"Oh, yes!" said the caterpillar in great excitement.

"Climb upon my back then, little caterpillar!" said the crafty bird.

The caterpillar did as he was told and the bird flew off towards his nest. At first the caterpillar clung tightly to the bird's back but soon he felt quite sleepy and eventually he dozed off and slipped from the bird's back. Down he fell through the air and landed on a leaf, but still he didn't wake up. Soon he was wrapped in a soft, brown, papery cocoon from which he would not wake up for a long while.

Meanwhile, the bird reached his nest. "Look at the treat I've brought you," he said to his chicks.

They looked very puzzled. "What treat, Dad?" one of them piped up.

"This nice juicy caterpillar," said the bird, shaking the feathers on his back. "Climb down, little caterpillar," he said. But of course there was nothing there. Now it was the father's turn to look puzzled, while the chicks laughed at him.

"Well, I must have dropped him," he said. "I've never done that before," he added. He flew out of the nest in search of the caterpillar but he was nowhere to be seen. Once he saw a strange brown, papery parcel on a leaf, but in the end the bird had to return to the nest with his beak empty.

A long while later the caterpillar woke up. "I must get out of this stuffy wrapping," he thought, as he pushed his way out.

He stood on the leaf and yawned and stretched. As he stretched, he noticed to his amazement two pairs of beautiful wings spreading out on either side of his body. "Are they really mine?" he wondered. He tried lifting and turning them and yes, he could make them work. He looked at his reflection in a raindrop and saw a lovely butterfly staring back at him. "So the ladybird and the bee were right," he exclaimed. "How foolish I was to be a jealous caterpillar," he declared to a passing ant, "for now I am a beautiful butterfly after all."

Maurice the Minnow's Dangerous Journey

Maurice the minnow lived in a beautiful, reed-fringed pond in a clearing in the middle of a small woodland. He had been born one fine spring morning, and now he spent each day swimming happily in the shallows with all his little minnow brothers and sisters.

But life in the pond had its dangers, too! He had heard alarming stories about a kingfisher that would dive into the water from a branch overhanging the pond and grab tiny fish and swallow them down. And then there was the heron – a great, grey, stalking bird that suddenly loomed into the shallows and snatched unsuspecting fish with its great beak.

But the stories Maurice feared most were the ones about Lucius the pike. Lucius had lived in the pond for longer than anyone could remember. Woe betide you if you met Lucius when he was hungry, for he would dart out from his hiding place among the water weeds, and you would be gone! Nothing ever escaped from his huge jaws, which were lined with needle-sharp teeth. Maurice had heard tales of Lucius swallowing fish bigger than Maurice could imagine – not to mention ducks, voles and other animals of the pond. Why, there was even a rumour that Lucius had once snatched a dog from the bank and taken it down to the depths of the pond to devour it!

Maurice's mother had said that the best way to avoid meeting Lucius was to always stay in the shallows, and never swim across the pond, for it was in the deep, dark waters that Lucius loved to hunt.

One sunny summer's day, Maurice and his brothers and sisters were swimming in the shallows as usual, when suddenly he felt himself being lifted up and out of the water. The next thing he knew he was flapping helplessly in the bottom of a net, gasping for breath. Mercifully, he soon found himself back in the water again, but it seemed different now. It was light all around and there were no welcoming, sheltering weeds to hide in. And where were all his brothers and sisters? Next, to his horror, he saw a huge, unfamiliar creature staring at him. He'd heard no stories about anything as big as this! The creature's head seemed so close that Maurice felt certain he was about to be eaten. But just as suddenly the creature seemed to move away, and Maurice felt himself being carried along in this new, strange, watery world.

Maurice was wondering if he was to be trapped in this new, small pond forever when just as suddenly as he seemed to have entered the pond, he was now leaving it again. He felt himself falling down, down, until – with a splash – he was back in his own pond again. Or at least, it seemed like his pond, but nothing was quite as familiar as it had been. Finding a clump of water weed, he immediately dived under it for safety, while he considered what to do next.

"Hello, you're new here, aren't you?" a friendly voice said. Maurice looked round in surprise to find himself face to face with a frog. He told the frog about his horrible adventure while the frog listened patiently, nodding wisely from time to time.

"Well, we know what's happened to you, don't we?" said the frog when Maurice had finished. "You got caught in a little boy's fishing net. They're often about around here. I've no doubt the big creature you saw was just the little boy looking at you swimming in his jam jar full of water. And now he's decided to put you back. The only trouble is, you're far from home. You live on the other side of the pond. And to get you back means we have got to go on a very dangerous journey."

Maurice didn't like the sound of this at all, but he missed his family terribly and knew that he would never be able to get back home without the kind frog's help. So without more ado, the two of them set off for their journey across the deep, dark pond.

"Swim near the surface. It's safer," advised the frog, "but keep a close eye out for kingfishers."

They seemed to have been swimming for ages, when suddenly a great, dark shadow appeared beneath them.

"It's Lucius!" cried the frog in fright.

Before either of them could escape, they found themselves face to face with the dreaded pike. "Well, well," leered Lucius. "I can't believe my luck! A frog *and* a minnow. Lunch and supper together if I'm not mistaken!"

So saying, he opened his enormous jaws and was about to swallow them whole when – BOINK! – a huge, flat stone landed right on Lucius's head. Dazed, Lucius sank slowly towards the bottom of the pond.

"Quick! It's our chance to escape!" yelled the frog. The two friends swam for their lives. Maurice kept thinking that any moment Lucius would reappear, but he needn't have worried. Lucius had too big a headache to think about hunting for a while yet!

Then suddenly Maurice was home. He recognised his own little part of the pond, and there swimming in the shallows was his family.

"I can't thank you enough," said Maurice gratefully to the frog. "But what *did* happen to Lucius?"

"You can thank the little boy who caught you in the net for our escape," said the frog. "He was skimming stones across the pond and luckily Lucius's head got in the way!"

Maurice decided that he'd had quite enough adventures for one day, and found himself a cosy piece of water weed to hide under. Soon he was fast asleep.